**Blastoff! Readers** are carefully developed by literacy experts to build reading stamina and move students toward fluency by combining standards-based content with developmentally appropriate text.

LEVELS

 **Level 1** provides the most support through repetition of high-frequency words, light text, predictable sentence patterns, and strong visual support.

 **Level 2** offers early readers a bit more challenge through varied sentences, increased text load, and text-supportive special features.

 **Level 3** advances early-fluent readers toward fluency through increased text load, less reliance on photos, advancing concepts, longer sentences, and more complex special features.

★ **Blastoff! Universe**

Reading Level

 Grade K →  Grades 1–3 →  Grade 4

This edition first published in 2025 by Bellwether Media, Inc.

No part of this publication may be reproduced in whole or in part without written permission of the publisher. For information regarding permission, write to Bellwether Media, Inc., Attention: Permissions Department, 6012 Blue Circle Drive, Minnetonka, MN 55343.

Library of Congress Cataloging-in-Publication Data

LC record for Switzerland available at: https://lccn.loc.gov/2024012117

Text copyright © 2025 by Bellwether Media, Inc. BLASTOFF! READERS and associated logos are trademarks and/or registered trademarks of Bellwether Media, Inc. Bellwether Media is a division of Chrysalis Education Group.

Editor: Suzane Nguyen   Designer: Laura Sowers

Printed in the United States of America, North Mankato, MN.

Table of Contents

All About Switzerland	4
Land and Animals	6
Life in Switzerland	12
Switzerland Facts	20
Glossary	22
To Learn More	23
Index	24

All About Switzerland

Bern

Switzerland is a small country in Europe. It is **landlocked**.

The capital is Bern.
The country is known for being beautiful and peaceful.

Land and Animals

Most of the country is covered in mountains. The Alps **range** has many **glaciers**.

The middle of the country is a **plateau**.

plateau

The Matterhorn

Size: 14,692 feet (4,478 meters) high
Famous For: one of the tallest and best-known mountains in the Alps

summer

Switzerland is a mostly **temperate** country. Summers are warm and wet. Snow falls in winter.

It is often colder in the mountains.

winter

Many animals live in the mountains. Alpine ibexes are goatlike animals. Red foxes run through the forests.

Alpine ibex

Marmots chirp near **meadows**. Wood nuthatches nest in trees.

Life in Switzerland

Most Swiss live in cities. German, Italian, French, and Romansch are mainly spoken.

Many people are **Christians**. Others do not practice religion.

alphorns

The Swiss enjoy keeping old **traditions**. They **yodel** and play alphorns.

Skiing and snowboarding are popular winter sports. People also enjoy mountain climbing.

mountain climbing

skiing

The Swiss love cheese!
Fondue is a popular dip.
Raclette is a melted cheese dish.

Swiss Foods

fondue

raclette

rösti

chocolate

chocolate

Rösti is fried shredded potatoes. Switzerland is also known for chocolate!

Fasnacht is a carnival at the beginning of **Lent**.

Swiss National Day is August 1. There are parades, costumes, and music. The Swiss love to **celebrate**!

Swiss National Day

Fasnacht

Switzerland Facts

Size:
15,937 square miles
(41,277 square kilometers)

Population:
8,563,760 (2023)

National Holiday:
Swiss National Day (August 1)

Main Languages:
French, German, Italian, Romansch

Capital City:
Bern

Famous Face

Name: Roger Federer

Famous For: former professional tennis player who won 20 Grand Slams

Religions

- other 9%
- Muslim 5%
- Catholic 34%
- Protestant 23%
- none 29%

Top Landmarks

Jet d'Eau fountain

Rhine Falls

Zytglogge clock tower

Glossary

celebrate—to do something special or fun for an event, occasion, or holiday

Christians—people who believe in the words of Jesus Christ

glaciers—massive sheets of ice that cover large areas of land

landlocked—enclosed or nearly enclosed by land

Lent—a period of 40 days when Christians prepare for Easter

meadows—lands that are covered, or mostly covered, with grass

plateau—an area of flat, raised land

range—a group of mountains

temperate—related to a mild climate that does not have extreme heat or cold

traditions—customs, ideas, or beliefs handed down from one generation to the next

yodel—to sing without words while going back and forth between one's natural voice and a higher voice

Index

alphorns, 14
Alps, 6, 7
animals, 10, 11
Bern, 4, 5
capital (see Bern)
Christians, 12
cities, 12
Europe, 4
Fasnacht, 18, 19
food, 16, 17
forests, 10
French, 12
German, 12, 13
glaciers, 6
Italian, 12
Lent, 18
map, 5
Matterhorn, 7
meadows, 11
mountain climbing, 15
mountains, 6, 7, 9, 10, 15
people, 12, 14, 15, 16, 18
plateau, 6
Romansch, 12
say hello, 13
skiing, 15
snow, 8
snowboarding, 15
summers, 8
Swiss National Day, 18
Switzerland facts, 20–21
winter, 8, 9, 15
yodel, 14

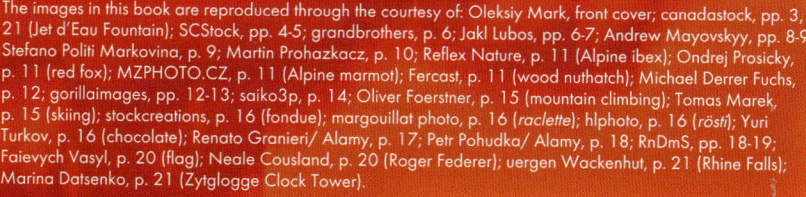

The images in this book are reproduced through the courtesy of: Oleksiy Mark, front cover; canadastock, pp. 3, 21 (Jet d'Eau Fountain); SCStock, pp. 4-5; grandbrothers, p. 6; Jakl Lubos, pp. 6-7; Andrew Mayovskyy, pp. 8-9; Stefano Politi Markovina, p. 9; Martin Prohazkacz, p. 10; Reflex Nature, p. 11 (Alpine ibex); Ondrej Prosicky, p. 11 (red fox); MZPHOTO.CZ, p. 11 (Alpine marmot); Fercast, p. 11 (wood nuthatch); Michael Derrer Fuchs, p. 12; gorillaimages, pp. 12-13; saiko3p, p. 14; Oliver Foerstner, p. 15 (mountain climbing); Tomas Marek, p. 15 (skiing); stockcreations, p. 16 (fondue); margouillat photo, p. 16 (*raclette*); hlphoto, p. 16 (*rösti*); Yuri Turkov, p. 16 (chocolate); Renato Granieri/ Alamy, p. 17; Petr Pohudka/ Alamy, p. 18; RnDmS, pp. 18-19; Faievych Vasyl, p. 20 (flag); Neale Cousland, p. 20 (Roger Federer); uergen Wackenhut, p. 21 (Rhine Falls); Marina Datsenko, p. 21 (Zytglogge Clock Tower).

To Learn More

AT THE LIBRARY

Duling, Kaitlyn. *Alpine Ibex*. Minneapolis, Minn.: Bellwether Media, 2021.

Sabelko, Rebecca. *Mountains*. Minneapolis, Minn.: Bellwether Media, 2022.

Spanier, Kristine. *Switzerland*. Minneapolis, Minn.: Jump!, 2020.

ON THE WEB

FACTSURFER

Factsurfer.com gives you a safe, fun way to find more information.

1. Go to www.factsurfer.com.
2. Enter "Switzerland" into the search box and click .
3. Select your book cover to see a list of related content.